To our little "Lockdown Baby"

Thank you for brightening up our world.

Lockdown Baby

Written by Laura Feldman
Illustrations by Svetlana Belova

First Printing, 2021

Published by Little Ivory Haus
www.ivoryhaus.com.au

ABN 59602478829

ISBN 978-0-6452568-2-6 Mother & Baby Hardcover
ISBN 978-0-6456809-6-6 Mother & Baby Paperback

Lockdown Baby

Written by Laura Feldman

Illustrations by Svetlana Belova

Dear little baby,
How we longed for you.
It started with a wish,
and in my tummy you grew.

After 9 months of growing
and wriggling away,
you finally arrived
on your special day.

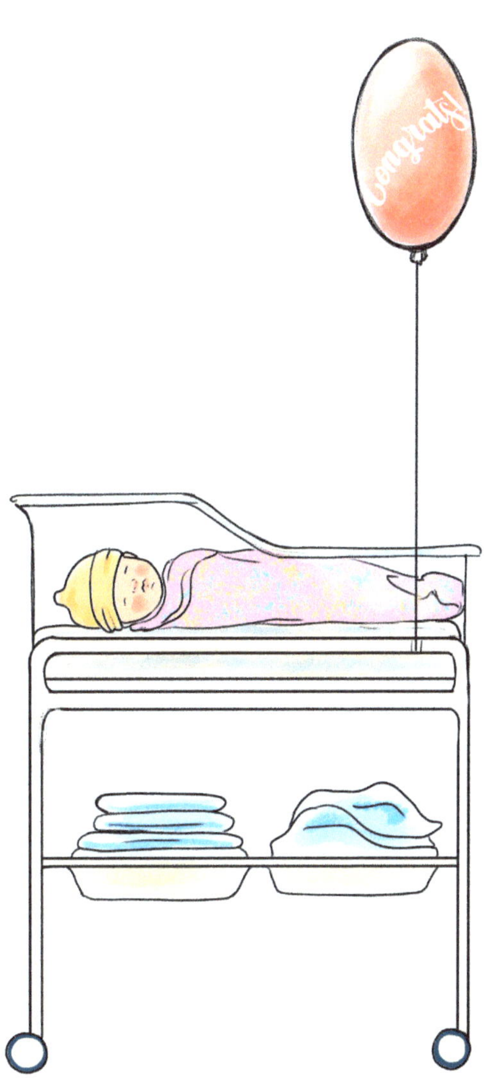
Congrats!

In hospital we snuggled
and got to know each other.
Whilst no visitors allowed,
it was a year like no other.

And then when we finally
got to go home,
you met all our friends
through a mobile phone.

Flowers and teddies
were left at the door,
blankets and clothes
and presents galore.

The people who love you
would coo from afar,
while wearing a mask
which might seem bizarre.

At times the shops
would suddenly shut...

And after watching the news,
we'd feel stuck in a rut.

It was all to keep you safe
so we didn't mind
that we stayed at home
all of the time.

One day you'll be bigger
and know what we mean
about this being a time
like we had never seen.

scanning
SAN

But even though some days were hard
and sometimes lonely too,
it didn't really matter much
because we now had you.

So now you're getting older,
and time goes by so fast,
we are so grateful for all the extra time
and memories made to last.

Our favourite lockdown memories...

www.ingramcontent.com/pod-product-compliance
Lightning Source LLC
LaVergne TN
LVHW070225110826
845147LV00003B/647

* 9 7 8 0 6 4 5 6 8 0 9 6 6 *